Jake at Gymnastics
Jake hace gimnasia

Rachel Isadora

Traducido por Teresa Mlawer

Nancy Paulsen Books 🌀 An Imprint of Penguin Group (USA)

NANCY PAULSEN BOOKS
Published by the Penguin Group
Penguin Group (USA) LLC
375 Hudson Street
New York, NY 10014

USA | Canada | UK | Ireland | Australia
New Zealand | India | South Africa | China
penguin.com
A Penguin Random House Company

Library of Congress Cataloging-in-Publication Data
Isadora, Rachel, author, illustrator.
Jake at gymnastics / Rachel Isadora.
pages cm
Summary: A group of toddlers has fun at gymnastics class.
[1. Toddlers—Fiction. 2. Gymnastics—Fiction.] I. Title.
PZ7.I763 Jak 2014
[E]—dc23
2013024243

Manufactured in China
ISBN 978-0-399-16048-6
Special Markets ISBN 978-0-399-54581-8 Not for Resale
3 5 7 9 10 8 6 4

Design by Marikka Tamura.
Text set in Rosemary.
The illustrations were done with pencil, ink, and oil paint on paper.

This Imagination Library edition is published by Penguin Young Readers, a division of
Penguin Random House, exclusively for Dolly Parton's Imagination Library, a not-for
-profit program designed to inspire a love of reading and learning, sponsored in part
by The Dollywood Foundation. Penguin's trade editions of this work are available
wherever books are sold.

For Nicholas

Para Nicholas

Jake says hello
to his friends and
his teacher, Dave.

Jake saluda a sus
amigos y a Dave,
su maestro.

Everyone is excited for gym
time to begin.

Todos están deseosos de que
comience la clase de gimnasia.

First we stretch on the mats.

Primero hacemos ejercicios de estiramiento en las colchonetas.

side split

apertura de
piernas lateral

**rotating
stretch**

rotación de
brazos

peekaboo

¿Cucú...? ¡Tras!

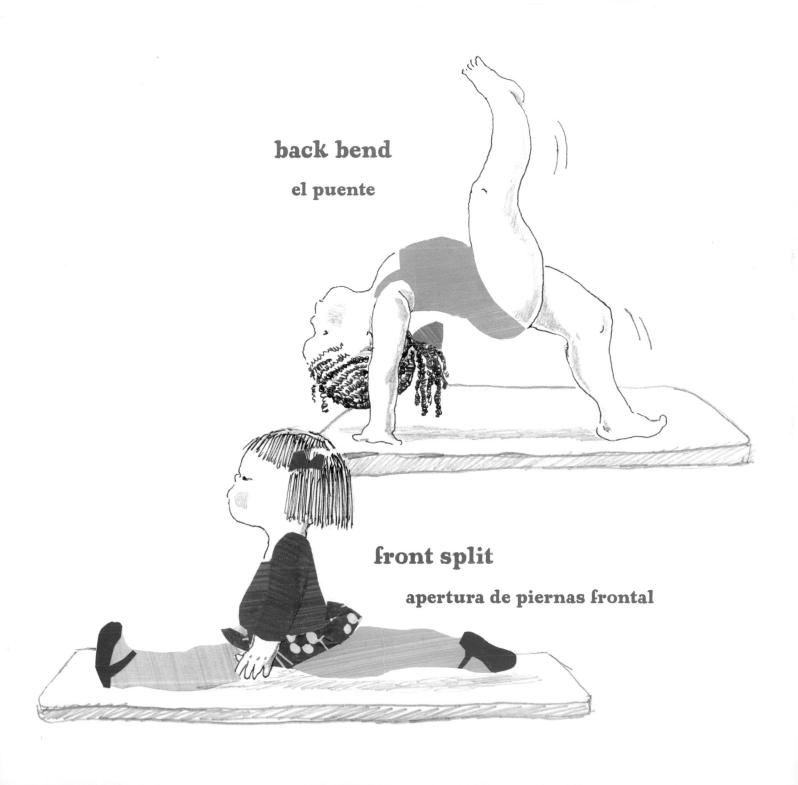

back bend

el puente

front split

apertura de piernas frontal

"Let's be frogs and hop today," Dave says.

—Hoy vamos a ser ranas y a saltar —dice Dave.

Maria crawls through the tunnel first.
María es la primera en gatear por el túnel.

Go, Maria!

¡Vamos, Maria!

Everyone follows.

Todos la siguen.

Then it's time for the balance beam.
Ahora toca la barra de equilibrio.

I'm doing it!
¡Puedo hacerlo!

Dave and his assistant, Toshi, help us on the low beam.

Dave y su asistente Toshi nos ayudan en la barra.

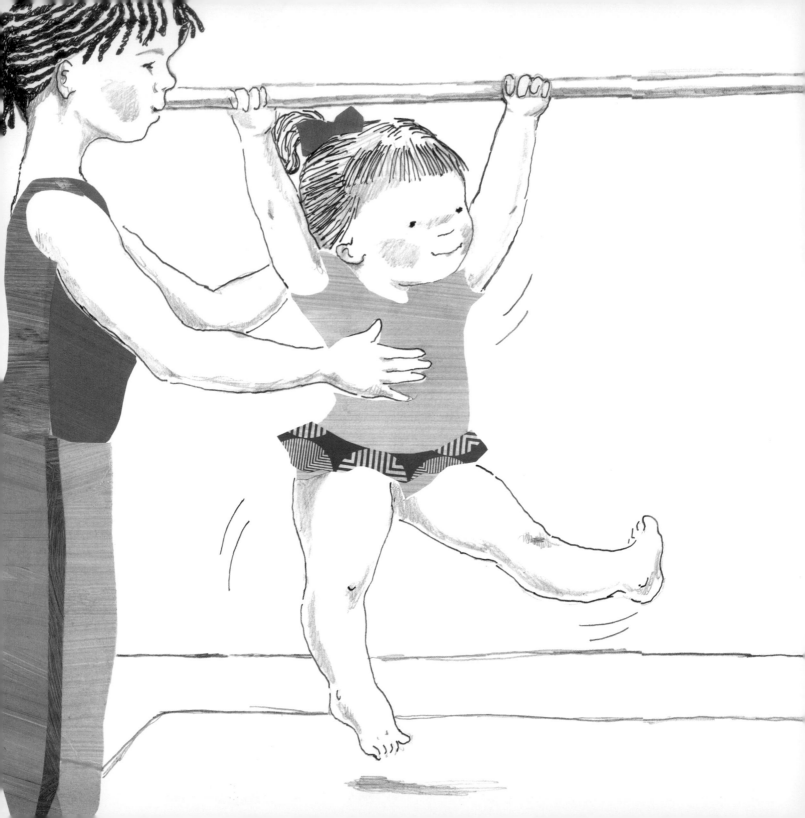

We try to
hang on to
the parallel bar
as long as
we can.

Tratamos de
mantenernos en
las barras paralelas
el mayor tiempo
posible.

It's fun to jump on the trampoline!

¡Qué divertido es saltar en el trampolín!

Jake swings high
on the rope.

Jake se columpia
alto en la cuerda.

Time to tumble.

Ahora toca rodar.

We all take turns doing somersaults.

Nos turnamos para dar volteretas.

Jake watches Laura do a handstand.

Jake observa a Laura
pararse de cabeza.

We bounce up and down on the bouncing balls.

Rebotamos arriba y abajo sobre las pelotas.

Everyone loves to jump barefoot into the ball pit.

A todos les gusta saltar descalzos en la piscina de bolas.

**Right before we go home,
Dave says, "Let's be birds."**

*—Antes de irnos a casa, vamos
a hacer como los pájaros —dice Dave.*

Tweet!
¡Pío, pío!

We spread our wings and
fly out the door.

Abrimos las alas y salimos
volando por la puerta.